I'm Going To R[...]

These levels are meant only as guides;
you and your child can best choose a book that's right.

Level 1: Kindergarten–Grade 1 . . . Ages 4–6
- word bank to highlight new words
- consistent placement of text to promote readability
- easy words and phrases
- simple sentences build to make simple stories
- art and design help new readers decode text

UP TO 50 WORDS

Level 2: Grade 1 . . . Ages 6–7
- word bank to highlight new words
- rhyming texts introduced
- more difficult words, but vocabulary is still limited
- longer sentences and longer stories
- designed for easy readability

UP TO 100 WORDS

Level 3: Grade 2 . . . Ages 7–8
- richer vocabulary of up to 200 different words
- varied sentence structure
- high-interest stories with longer plots
- designed to promote independent reading

UP TO 200 WORDS

Level 4: Grades 3 and up . . . Ages 8 and up
- richer vocabulary of more than 300 different words
- short chapters, multiple stories, or poems
- more complex plots for the newly independent reader
- emphasis on reading for meaning

MORE THAN 300 WORDS

LEVEL 3

Library of Congress Cataloging-in-Publication Data Available

2 4 6 8 10 9 7 5 3

Published by Sterling Publishing Co., Inc.
387 Park Avenue South, New York, NY 10016
Text copyright © 2007 by Harriet Ziefert Inc.
Illustrations copyright © 2007 by Yukiko Kido
Distributed in Canada by Sterling Publishing
c/o Canadian Manda Group, 165 Dufferin Street
Toronto, Ontario, Canada M6K 3H6
Distributed in the United Kingdom by GMC Distribution Services,
Castle Place, 166 High Street, Lewes, East Sussex, England BN7 1XU
Distributed in Australia by Capricorn Link (Australia) Pty. Ltd.
P.O. Box 704, Windsor, NSW 2756, Australia

Printed in China

Sterling ISBN 13: 978-1-4027-4246-0
ISBN 10: 1-4027-4246-0

For information about custom editions, special sales, premium and
corporate purchases, please contact Sterling Special Sales
Department at 800-805-5489 or specialsales@sterlingpub.com.

I'm Going To READ!

A DOZEN DOZENS

Pictures by Yukiko Kido

Sterling Publishing Co., Inc.
New York

What is a dozen?

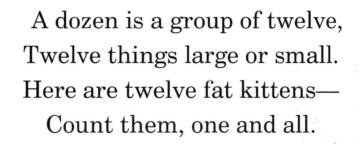

A dozen is a group of twelve,
Twelve things large or small.
Here are twelve fat kittens—
Count them, one and all.

What is a half dozen? . . . . .

Let's count up half a dozen.
That's six of anything:
Six tulips or six roses—
They smell just like spring.

A dozen eggs are in the barn.
Six of them have cracks.
Two chicks are peeking out,
Their shells still on their backs.

I love a yummy cherry pie.
My sister Sue likes peach.
Altogether we have twelve—
Or half a dozen each.

Half a dozen apples,
Half a dozen more.
I've got a dozen apples
Inside my desk drawer.

If I had two dozen feet,
I'd need twelve pairs of socks.

I'd fold them all up neatly
In a big blue box.

My father ate two slices.
My mother wanted three.
My sister wanted only one,
Leaving six for me!

Twelve big goldfish
Swimming in a school.
Guess how many goldfish
Will be left in the pool?

Dog has eleven cousins.
He's one of a dozen.

Do you know anybody
With so many cousins?

Mary has quadruplets.
Her brother Tom has twins.

That's half a dozen babies
With banana on their chins.

These two sets of triplets
Belong to Suzy Jane.
That's half a dozen kids
Walking in the rain.

Half a dozen acrobats,
Twelve legs in the air . . .

Another half a dozen,
Balanced on a chair!

FAMILY MATH FUN

- In your house, are there a dozen

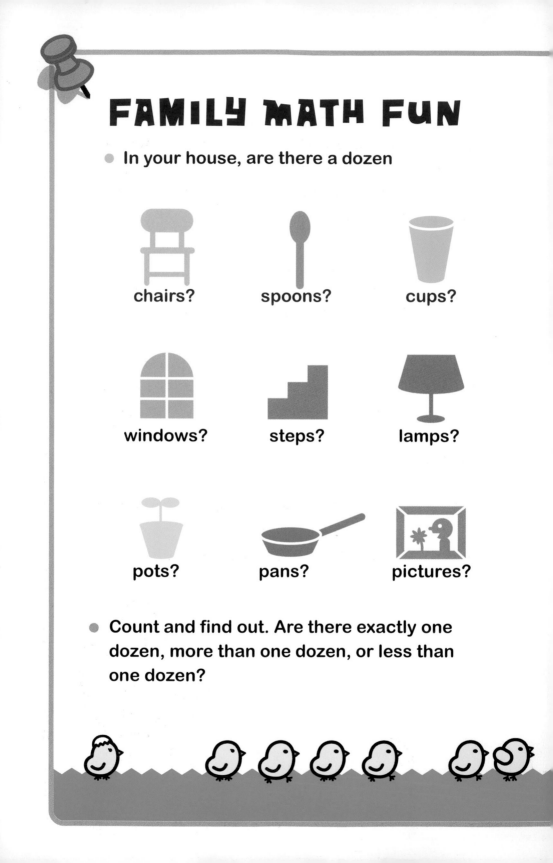

chairs? spoons? cups?

windows? steps? lamps?

pots? pans? pictures?

- Count and find out. Are there exactly one dozen, more than one dozen, or less than one dozen?

- Do you know the names of a dozen different kinds of dinosaurs? Make a list of the ones you know, then ask a grown-up to help you until your list has twelve kinds. You can also try to list a dozen kinds of dogs, bugs, or birds.

- Write a story about a dozen bugs, or a dozen dogs, or a dozen cats, or a dozen dinosaurs. Make a picture to go with the words.

- Do you have a dozen of anything? What? If you don't, perhaps you would like to collect a dozen rocks, or a dozen stamps, or a dozen acorns, or a dozen pennies, or a dozen marbles.

- Look in the telephone book. Are there a dozen families with the same last name as yours? More than a dozen? Less than a dozen?